BIONICLE®

Maze
of Shadows

BIONICLE®

*FIND THE POWER,
LIVE THE LEGEND*

The legend comes alive in these exciting BIONICLE® books:

BIONICLE™ Chronicles

#1 Tale of the Toa
#2 Beware the Bohrok
#3 Makuta's Revenge
#4 Tales of the Masks

The Official Guide to BIONICLE™

BIONICLE™ Collector's Sticker Book

BIONICLE™ Mask of Light

BIONICLE® Adventures

#1 Mystery of Metru Nui
#2 Trial by Fire
#3 The Darkness Below
#4 Legends of Metru Nui
#5 Voyage of Fear

BIONICLE®

Maze of Shadows

by Greg Farshtey

SCHOLASTIC INC.
New York Toronto London Auckland Sydney
Mexico City New Delhi Hong Kong Buenos Aires

*For Jeff, a noble soul
and a true friend*

ISBN 0-439-68023-9

© 2004 The LEGO Group. LEGO, the LEGO logo, BIONICLE, and the BIONICLE logo are registered trademarks of The LEGO Group and are used here by special permission. All rights reserved. Published by Scholastic Inc. SCHOLASTIC and associated logos are trademarks and/or registered trademarks of Scholastic Inc.

12 11 10 9 8 7 6 5 4 3 2   4 5 6 7 8/0

Printed in the U.S.A.
First printing, December 2004

INTRODUCTION

Turaga Nuju walked alone down a winding, rocky pathway that led to the sea. He had no doubt he would find Vakama on the beach, gazing out at the horizon. For a Turaga of Fire, Vakama spent an awful lot of time by the water.

Nuju felt uncomfortable. Ordinarily, he never ventured forth without Matoro, his assistant and translator, by his side. In the centuries since Nuju had abandoned use of the Matoran language, Matoro's full-time job had been rendering the Turaga's speech understandable to others. The Matoran had been present for even the most confidential councils of the Turaga. He had heard things that must have shocked him. But he never repeated a word of what he had heard to anyone.

Matoro's sense of duty to his Turaga was so strong that he never even asked why Nuju was going somewhere without him. Perhaps he realized it was not intended as any insult, but was rather an act of mercy on Nuju's part.

He carries a heavy burden, thought the Turaga. *To know so many secrets and be forbidden to share them with his friends, even when that knowledge might benefit them. In that way, Matoro has the strength of a Toa. I will not add to his burden today.*

Nuju came over a rise and saw Vakama standing at the edge of the sea. For the last several days, the elder of the village of Fire had been sharing tales of the past with the Toa Nuva. He had related how six Matoran were mysteriously turned into heroes, the Toa Metru, and fought to save their city of Metru Nui. When the city was badly damaged and its population cast into an endless sleep by the actions of the evil Makuta, the Toa Metru had escaped with a small number of Matoran and made it to this island.

But the Toa Nuva were not satisfied with

what they had learned. They wanted to know how the rest of the Matoran escaped Metru Nui. And Vakama was preparing to tell them.

Up to now, I have been content to let him share his tales, thought Nuju. *But he is about to go too far.*

The Turaga of Ice stalked across the sand, whistling and chirping angrily. Vakama turned, surprised, and held out his hands.

"Slow down," he said. "You know I can't understand you when you shout."

Nuju made a series of violent slashing motions in the air, followed by a short burst of whistles. When he was finished, he glared at Vakama as if daring him to disagree.

"I know it is probably not wise," the Turaga of Fire answered. "I am on the verge of sharing stories of a time we would all rather forget, myself most of all. But wisdom and necessity often do not walk side by side."

Nuju chirped loudly five times in rapid succession. To anyone else, it would have sounded like the language of the birds in the trees of Le-Wahi. But Vakama knew the tone was one of frustration about to boil over.

"No one says you and the other Turaga must sit in council while I tell our story," he said. "But you may be called upon to explain your absence someday."

The Turaga of Ice picked up a rock and hurled it with all his might into the water. Then he walked away, eyes on the ground, as if wrestling with an enormously difficult decision.

When he turned back, Nuju looked directly into Vakama's eyes. And for the first time that Vakama could remember in many, many years, Nuju spoke a Matoran word. It was a mere three syllables, but it was a terrible sound, a word not uttered by any Turaga in over a thousand years.

"Hordika."

Vakama's reply was a whisper. "Yes. If I must . . . the Toa Nuva will learn the truth about the Hordika."

Nuju shook his head and walked away.

Vakama was left behind to wonder if their friendship had just come to an end.

The Toa Nuva waited impatiently around the Amaja circle for Vakama to arrive. At the Turaga's request, the only Matoran present were Matoro, who translated Nuju's clicks and whistles into speech, and Hahli, in her role as the new Chronicler. Takanuva, Toa of Light, sat next to Hahli, looking uncomfortable. Not having been a Toa for very long, he still felt strange about being part of these councils.

Pohatu Nuva, Toa of Stone, noted that his Turaga was absent. He couldn't imagine why Onewa would not have wanted to be here, or why Turaga Nuju sat apart from the other elders. But it seemed that ever since Vakama had promised to share at least one more tale, there had been a great strain among the Turaga. It filled Pohatu's heart with apprehension. What were they about to hear?

Vakama stepped out of the shadows to take his seat. Yet, to Pohatu's eyes, it seemed he did not leave the darkness completely behind. His mood was grim. He nodded to Tahu Nuva, but never once looked at the other Turaga.

"Hear, then, my tale," he began softly. "When the Toa Metru first beheld the island we now call Mata Nui, it was like nothing we had ever seen before. Peaceful, beautiful, bathed in sunlight, we could not have hoped for a more wonderful home.

"But even as we explored, we knew that duty would soon require us to leave this place behind . . ."

Toa Matau had a secret, one he had not even wanted to admit to himself. It was a dark and shameful fact, something he hoped none of the other Toa Metru would ever learn: He had gotten lost.

For a native of Le-Metru, transport hub of Metru Nui, to lose his way was completely humiliating. A Le-Matoran could track a chute from one end of the city to the other, or keep an airship on course just by spotting landmarks far below. And now here was the Toa Metru of Air, already wandering and confused after only a day in this new land!

It had started out simply enough. Each of the Toa Metru had gone in a different direction, looking for the best place to eventually settle their metru's Matoran. Only Nokama had remained behind, content that their original landing spot was the best place for a new Ga-Metru. Matau had made immediately for a lush, green part of the island. To him, it seemed to most resemble the controlled chaos that was Le-Metru.

As it turned out, "chaos" was accurate, "controlled" was not. The ground was soft and clung to his feet, making walking a chore. The ceiling of branches was so thick that he could not fly through it. Worse, it cut off the sunlight, making the journey akin to wandering through an Onu-Metru mine.

Then Matau saw reason to smile. He spotted what looked like a long, green cable with a red stripe down the side, similar to the ones that fed magnetic force into Metru Nui chutes. Any native of Le-Metru knew that following a cable would eventually lead to a control center. So Matau kept his eye on the cable as it snaked through the tangle overhead, traveling deeper and deeper into the heart of the jungle. Confident that this clue would lead somewhere worthwhile, the Toa paid little attention to where he was going or how far he had walked.

After a few hours, he reached the end of the cable. But the discovery he made was an unpleasant one: It wasn't a Metru Nui force wire, it was a vine. It didn't lead to chute controls or anything like that, but just to more trees. Now here he stood, lost in a dense jungle and unsure what would be worse, roaming around with no idea how to get out or having to shout for help.

This is not Metru Nui. It will never be Metru Nui, he said to himself. *I had better start remembering that.*

Nuju stood at the summit of a huge mountain, looking out over a snow-covered land. He had been intrigued to discover that the peak was not made of crystal, like the Knowledge Towers back home, but was rather rock covered with ice.

He triggered the telescopic lens built into his Mask of Power to take a closer look at his surroundings. He was at a loss to explain the varied terrains and climates present on this island. It was almost as if the island had evolved with the needs of the Matoran in mind.

Down below, he spotted a snowfield protected from the worst of the elements by an overhanging glacier. *This,* he decided, *would be the perfect spot for a new Ko-Metru. Although, since it will be more a village than a part of a larger city,* he noted, *perhaps Ko-Koro would be a more accurate name.*

Satisfied, he began the long trek down the side of the mountain. As he did, he remembered the words of the Ko-Matoran sage who had first recruited him for work in the Knowledge Towers. Nuju had been wondering how long it might take him to become a seer, a position of great importance in Ko-Metru. His mentor had simply smiled.

"You are mistaken, Nuju," he had said. "All of life is a journey, and the journey is not about how high you climb or how far you walk. It is about what you learn on the way, and how you choose to use that knowledge. Use it to help others, and the glory of Mata Nui will live inside you. Use it only for yourself, and though you may walk among us, you will have no more spirit than a block of protodermis."

My journey has certainly taken some unexpected turns, thought Nuju. *And none quite so overwhelming as this, having to build a civilization from a wilderness. But the words of my mentor will be my guide. And if I should forget them, this peak will serve to remind me.*

Nuju turned and looked back up at the summit. "In the memory of a friend, who now sleeps the sleep of shadows," he said to the mountain, "I give to you his name. From this day on, you will be Mount Ihu."

Vakama moved carefully across a sea of molten protodermis. His eyes scanned the landscape with a very particular goal in mind, one that went far beyond simply the best spot for a new settlement.

He paused on a rocky ledge and pondered. He and Onewa had discussed at length what life might be like on this island in the years to come.

Neither Toa Metru believed they had seen the last of Makuta. Even if they succeeded in bringing the Matoran from Metru Nui to this place, and somehow awakening them, they might still never know peace. If Makuta escaped the prison they had created for him, he would not stop his efforts to dominate the Matoran.

That was why, when Vakama looked around, he did not see simply rock and fire. He saw points of vulnerability that would need to be better protected, perhaps by walls or a moat of some sort. He noted spots that could be easily defended, even by only a few well-trained Matoran. By combining the natural terrain with the ingenuity of Ta-Matoran, Vakama was sure he could create much more than a village.

This will be a fortress, he told himself, *one whose gates will never be breached. The Matoran will learn how to do the job of the Vahki, defending their homes against any threat.*

Even as he thought those words, pain ripped through his mind. It was another of his visions of the future. They had plagued him all his life, but had grown worse since he became a Toa Metru. This time, it produced not so much a visual image as a feeling, as if he were being drained of all energy. It passed quickly, but not before he realized exactly what it was he was experiencing: the loss of his Toa power.

Even after so long, Vakama was unsure just how accurate his visions might be. But if this one was true — if, somehow, he and possibly the other Toa Metru were going to cease to be Toa — then something would have to be done to insure the safety of the Matoran.

But it will not be easy, he knew. *And it will not be something I can do alone.*

He fitted his disk launcher on his back and mentally triggered its rocket pack function. Then Vakama soared into the sky and headed for the rendezvous point, wondering how he would convince his friends that their time as Toa might soon come to an end.

Onewa was pleased. He had succeeded in finding a portion of this island that closely resembled

Po-Metru. There was plenty of room for a village and scores of caves in which carvings could be stored. The natural canyons would give the new Po-Metru some protection and be a reminder of home for the Matoran.

Now he had more practical matters to worry about. In order to escape the Vahki, Onewa had been forced to use his power to destroy the subterranean waterway that led from Metru Nui to the island. A rain of stone had been enough to down the order enforcement squad, but it had also effectively blocked the Toa Metru from ever returning to the city that way. If they were going to go back and save the rest of the Matoran, a new route would have to be found.

The caves are the key, he thought. *Who knows how far underground they might extend? It's always possible that one of these leads all the way back to Metru Nui, and if so I'm going to find it.*

He chose to first explore a cavern whose mouth was high up on the slope of a mountain. He had thought to take one of the lightstones from the transport. Now it provided a dim illumination as he entered the cave.

It was empty. There were no signs that anyone had ever passed through here before, nor that any Rahi had ever made it his home. After only a short distance, the ground began to drop sharply. Onewa smiled. Down was exactly where he was hoping to go, after all.

He heard a scuffling sound up ahead. Something large was heading toward him at a rapid pace. Onewa glanced around, but there were no side passages or recesses in the wall in which to take cover. Whatever was coming, he would have to face it head on.

The Toa of Stone braced himself and held up his lightstone. The sounds grew louder. Suddenly, a massive shape came into view, claws and stinger-tail gleaming in the light of the crystal. Onewa gasped. It was a Nui-Jaga, one of the nastier Rahi of Po-Metru, a powerful scorpion-like creature capable of shattering a stone sculpture with one swipe of its tail.

Onewa forced himself to relax. His Kanohi mask was designed for just this sort of situation. He reached out with its power of mind control to take over the Nui-Jaga.

The Toa reeled as if he had been struck with a hurled boulder. His mental probe had slammed into a solid wall of raw emotion in the mind of the Rahi. The impact shattered the efforts of the mask to claim control of the Nui-Jaga and it was only with supreme effort that Onewa remained conscious.

The Rahi now had the perfect opening to attack. Instead, it rushed past Onewa, knocking him off his feet, and continued to race for the surface. Recovering his wits, the Toa pursued. He was amazed that something as big as a Nui-Jaga could move so fast.

Onewa rounded a corner to see the creature rushing toward the cave mouth. Without slowing, without making any effort at all to stop, the Rahi shot out of the tunnel and plunged into space. The Toa made it to the opening in time to see the Nui-Jaga strike the rocky ground far below. There was no need to go down and check the body. The Rahi was dead.

I've never seen anything like that, Onewa thought. *What could have made it run so hard it went off a cliff?*

Then he remembered the overwhelming surge of feeling he had encountered when he reached into the Rahi's mind. That held the answer, or at least part of one. It hadn't been anger, or hunger, or even madness that had driven the Nui-Jaga to race to its death.

It had been stark terror.

Onewa glanced down at the stone resting at his feet. Then he looked back at Vakama.

"You realize, of course, that you are completely insane, fire-spitter," he said.

The Toa Metru had assembled on the beach where they had first come ashore. Matau had been the last to arrive, for reasons he refused to explain. When they reached the rendezvous point, they found that Vakama was already there and had placed six stones in a circle in the sand.

No one needed to be told what they were meant to be. Each of them recalled the day Toa Lhikan visited six Matoran in Metru Nui and handed them Toa stones. Lhikan had invested each of the stones with some of his Toa power. It was that power that had turned the Matoran into the Toa Metru they were today. But sharing his power had resulted in Lhikan transforming from a Toa into a smaller, weaker Turaga.

"Forget this thought-plan," said Matau. "I am a Toa-hero, and I intend to stay a Toa-hero."

"Keep calm," said Nokama. "No one is being forced to do anything. Let's hear Vakama out."

As briefly as possible, the Toa of Fire explained his vision. Nokama, Nuju, and Whenua listened attentively, but gave no indication whether they believed him or not. Matau shrugged. Onewa turned away, shaking his head.

Vakama hurled a ball of fire in the Toa of Stone's path. Angry, Onewa whirled back around, but Vakama cut him off before he could speak. "This is important! Whether the feeling I had means anything or not, we are not immortals.

18

What if one or all of us should die trying to rescue the Matoran? Shouldn't we act to insure that other Toa can follow us someday?"

"But past experience says that if we put our power into those stones, we will become Turaga," said Whenua. "Then who will there be to save the Matoran?"

"I'm not becoming a Turaga," Matau insisted. "I will swing from the trees like a Rahi first."

"Lhikan invested his energy into *six* stones," said Vakama, picking up one of the perfectly smooth rocks. "Each of us will put a portion of ours into only one. Then we will hide them on this island, in places that only someone with the heart of a true Toa could ever reach."

None of the Toa Metru said anything. Vakama looked from one to the other, searching for some show of support. Finding none, he placed the stone in the palm of his left hand and then held his right hand over it. Concentrating, he sent a fraction of his Toa power into the stone. It was a strange and unsettling experience.

It felt as if the rock was actually hungry for his energy. Only with a supreme act of will was Vakama able to break off the transfer before he had surrendered too much power.

Nokama waited until Vakama was done. Then she bent down and picked up her stone. A moment later, Nuju and Whenua followed suit. Then all three looked at Matau.

"Fine," said the Toa of Air, snatching up the stone and tossing it from hand to hand. "But no other Toa-hero will want to follow me. How could another ever compare?"

Only the Toa of Stone still stood apart. Nokama picked up Onewa's Toa stone and held it out to him. "The Toa need to be six united. Air, fire, water, earth, ice . . . what are we without the strength of stone?"

Onewa took the small rock from her hand. "All right," he said. "I'll do it because you ask, Nokama."

The Toa of Fire reached out and grabbed Onewa's wrist. Their eyes locked as Vakama, in a voice as hard as solid protodermis, said, "No. You will do it because it is the right thing to do."

Onewa shook off Vakama's grip. "All right, all right. Who died and made you Mata Nui anyway?"

"No one," said Vakama softly. "And I am going to make sure no one ever does."

Hiding the six Toa stones took a good part of the rest of the day. Most of the Toa Metru used it as an excuse to do more exploring. Matau, who had already had quite enough of trees, vines, and swamps, grumbled that after all this it would probably be some curious Matoran who stumbled on them by accident. "No heart of a true Toa-hero needed," he muttered. "Just feet that want to wander."

After he had found a suitable place to stash the stone, Matau scrambled to the top of a tree and launched himself into the sky. His destination was Po-Wahi, the barren, stony area Onewa had claimed as his own. From high above, he could see the other Toa making their way to the same spot, each in their own way. For a moment, he considered challenging Nuju to a race, ice slide versus glider wings. Then he suddenly realized that would involve asking the Toa of Ice to do something *fun*.

This place is making me thought-crazy, he said to himself.

Onewa was standing at the opening of a cave when the other Toa arrived. Knowing they would ask, he hurriedly explained about the dead Nui-Jaga at the bottom of the slope. "If a Rahi could get up here from Metru Nui, it stands to reason that we can get back the same way," he concluded. "And I think we should get started, before more start showing up."

As usual, Whenua was put out front for the journey, since his Mask of Night Vision could light the way. He paused for a moment at the cave's mouth, gloomily surveying the rock walls within. "Tunnels. Why does it always have to be tunnels?"

"Tell you what," said Matau, smiling. "I will wear the torch-mask and explore the tunnels from now on, and you can live in the mud-swamp. What do you say?"

"I say there's nothing like a good tunnel," Whenua replied, leading the way inside.

They had been journeying only a short while when Whenua called for a halt. "There's a cavern up ahead, and I thought I saw . . ."

The Toa of Earth's voice trailed off as the light from his mask played across the cave. Arrayed against the walls were hundreds of cyclinders, each containing a sleeping Bohrok. Whenua had seen the creatures before in the Metru Nui Archives, but only Onu-Matoran miners had ever seen them in their nest. The sight managed to be fascinating and deeply disturbing at the same time.

"I never liked those things," Matau shuddered. "Let's move quick-fast and not wake them up."

Recovered from his surprise, Whenua walked up to one of the cylinders and slammed his earthshock drill against it. The resulting clang echoed throughout the tunnels, but that was the only effect. The Bohrok inside never stirred.

"I don't think they can awaken, at least not in

the sense you mean," said the Toa of Earth. "Miners have transported them up several levels to the Archives and they have never flickered to life."

"So they are dead?" asked Nokama, keeping her distance from the nest.

"Sleeping," corrected Nuju. "Waiting for the day they will be needed, though I cannot imagine what crisis would require their services."

"It's funny," said Vakama, approaching one of the cylinders. "These remind me of the spheres the Matoran are trapped in down below, sleeping their dreamless sleep. Do you think that perhaps —"

The rest of his question was never voiced. No sooner had his hand brushed the cylinder than a vision exploded in his head. He saw hundreds, thousands of Bohrok rampaging across the island above, destroying forests, mountains, and rivers. Natural features that had stood for ages were swept away in an instant. When the swarms were done, they left behind a ravaged land.

"No . . . no . . ." Vakama moaned. "It must not be . . ."

"What is it?" Nokama asked urgently. "Speak to us."

"The Bohrok. One day, they will awaken and Mata Nui will fall before them . . . I saw it!"

"These things?" said Onewa, laughing. "They do nothing but sleep! What are they going to do, snore Mata Nui to death?"

"Vakama's visions have been correct before," Nokama reminded him.

"Vakama's visions should be carved onto a tablet and titled, 'Tales to Frighten Matoran'," Onewa shot back. "Just because he accurately guessed that a rampaging plant might be a bad thing in Metru Nui doesn't mean — owww!"

Onewa jumped back. He had been struck by a drop of liquid that had fallen from the ceiling. Now it sizzled on the surface of his armor. "Makuta's eyes, what was that?"

Whenua turned to look. The light from his mask revealed a rivulet of silver liquid flowing from the tunnel ceiling down to a small pool at the base of the wall. At first, he thought it was simply liquid protodermis, but the color and texture seemed slightly off. He leaned down to touch the substance, but Nuju stopped him.

"Not a good idea, librarian," the Toa of Ice said. "If that is what I think it is, touching it is the last thing you want to do."

Nuju knelt down to examine the pool. The other Toa crowded around him. "Nokama, you know, don't you? The labs in Ga-Metru were trying to produce this based on ancient records in the Knowledge Towers."

"Energized protodermis," Nokama said, awe in her voice. "Yes, some were trying to reproduce it, but with no success. I never thought I would see the real thing."

"What is it?" asked Vakama. "An acid?"

"More than that," Nuju replied. "If the tablets are to be believed, energized protodermis can produce mutations of the most bizarre kinds. Under the right circumstances, a being exposed to it could be physically changed, granted new powers, or possibly turned into some sort of monster. There's no way to predict its effects."

Matau smiled. "So if I took a quick-swim, I could come out as a new kind of Toa?"

"If it was your destiny," said Nuju. "If not . . ."

A stone rat scurried across the tunnel floor. It paused for an instant at the sight of the Toa, then darted around them and right into the pool. There was a horrible hissing sound. The small creature struggled to free itself from the liquid, but the protodermis clung to it like a second skin. Then the rat spasmed, smoke rising from its body. Before the horrified eyes of the Toa, the small creature dissolved, leaving no trace it had ever been there.

"The secret of energized protodermis," Nuju said quietly. "What it doesn't transform . . . it destroys."

No one spoke for a long time.

Nokama walked beside Vakama. The Toa of Fire's expression was grim. He had already prevented Whenua from investigating two new species of Rahi, and snapped at Matau for lagging behind. Nokama had never seen him act quite this way.

"Is anything the matter?" she asked gently.

"We are not making this trip for pleasure," he replied. "But it seems some of us don't realize that. The longer it takes us to reach the city, the greater the chance that some new danger will threaten the Matoran."

"You mean Makuta might free himself?" The Toa Metru had left their nemesis trapped in solid protodermis marked with a Toa seal. In theory, only the powers of the six Toa could release him.

"He might," Vakama acknowledged. "Or there might be worse things than Makuta. I don't know. But it seems obvious we will never get there without someone acting as leader."

"You always said you didn't want that role."

"I didn't want to see my friends and my Turaga trapped, or my city wrecked, either," he answered, never taking his eyes from the path ahead. "But I did."

Yes, you did, Nokama thought. *And it has changed you. But for the better . . . or for the worse?*

* * *

Matau had caught up to Whenua. Bored, the Toa of Air was using his Mask of Power to shapeshift into whatever came to mind, much to his friend's annoyance.

"So how did you like the island?" Matau asked while in the shape of a Kikanalo beast.

"Good, deep soil and rock," Whenua answered. "Perfect for digging."

"Yes, that's what I look for in a home, too," Matau answered, wondering if perhaps Onu-Matoran had something wrong behind their masks. *Why would anyone want to live underground when they could have the sky?*

"How about you?"

Matau shrugged, shifting to a copy of the late Dark Hunter named Krekka. "Mud-swamp. Thorn-vines. Too much mud for riding, too many trees for flying. It needs work."

"I am sure the Le-Matoran will manage," Whenua answered. "If you can't build chutes, you can always swing from the vines."

"Right," snorted Matau. "Good happy-joke."

Whenua's foot slipped. He stuck a hand out barely in time to keep from falling. He looked down at his feet, the beam from his mask illuminating a coating of fine-grained sand on the tunnel floor.

"That's odd. We are a long way from any beach. How did sand get here?"

There was a blur of motion. The sand whipped itself into a storm in the narrow passage. For a moment, Matau thought he spotted a shape in the center of the cyclone. Then both he and Whenu were sent flying by hammerlike blows.

Matau struck the tunnel wall hard enough to rattle his mask. He decided the impact was making him see things. There couldn't really be a Kranua, armor gleaming in the light of Whenua's mask, blocking their path . . . could there?

Kranua were a special model of Vahki, built in secret by Nuparu and a select crew of Po-Matoran engineers. Their intended purpose was riot control, in particular containing mass Rahi breakouts from the Archives. Their designers had given them the ability to reduce their forms to a mass of sandy protodermis grains, and then re-form at will. This allowed them to slip through tiny cracks, vanish through gratings, and then suddenly reappear when least expected. In practice, the Kranua were used against Matoran smuggling rings and other organized groups of lawbreakers, which always seemed to Matau like swatting a fireflyer with a two-ton rock.

Now the massive order enforcer was standing square in their way. It hadn't moved forward to press its advantage, but it showed no signs of stepping aside either. Cautiously, Matau glanced over at Whenua. The Toa of Earth was still stunned. That left it up to him.

Slowly, carefully, Matau got to his feet. "Pleasant day for a slow-walk," he began, taking a step forward. "My friends and I are just passing through. Is this your tunnel-home?"

Matau edged toward the Kranua's left side.

The elite Vahki's head moved to track the Toa, its attention drawn away from Whenua. When he was sure he had the thing's full attention, Matau leapt toward the tunnel ceiling as if making a break for it. The Kranua shifted its body to sand, not knowing it was falling into a trap.

The Toa of Air launched a wind blast at the Vahki, scattering its grains all over the tunnel. Matau grabbed Whenua and hauled him to his feet. "Come on, while the sand-thing is busy, we have to tell the others!"

They turned and ran back the way they had come, but made it only a few steps. A wall of sand as hard as stone suddenly loomed before them. Then it dissolved into a tidal wave, burying the two Toa and cutting off their air. Blinded and suffocating, Matau and Whenua lashed out, only to find there was nothing substantial to hit.

Desperate, Matau unleashed his power. His winds slammed into the Kranua, but instead of providing the Toa relief, all they did was transform their enemy into a sandstorm. Worse, it seemed that Matau and Whenua were caught in the cyclone as well, for they were lifted off the ground and sent flying.

The two Toa Metru crashed to earth at the feet of Nuju. "Travel by telekinesis — a new method even for you, Matau," said the Toa of Ice.

"You need long-work on your landings," groaned Matau.

Vakama and Onewa stood side by side, watching the Kranua coalesce. "I worked on one of those things," said the Toa of Stone. "It's slow, but a lot stronger than your average Vahki."

"That's all right," said Vakama. "So are we. Give it something to think about, Onewa."

Concentrating his power on the rock wall, Onewa tore a stone loose by force of mind and sent it hurtling at the Kranua. Spotting the danger, the complex machine transformed itself to soft sand to let the object pass through. As soon as it did, Vakama sent an intense blast of flame into the tunnel, so hot and bright it sent Onewa stumbling backwards.

When the Toa of Stone could see clearly again, an incredible sight greeted his eyes. The Kranua, caught in mid-transformation by Vakama's fires, had been fused into a statue of glass. Now it stood, unmoving, looking like some sculptor's nightmare. The other Toa moved in closely to examine it, but Vakama was already moving deeper into the tunnel.

"Leave it," he said. "It's not going anywhere."

Whenua watched him go, muttering to no one in particular, "Ever wonder why he needs us?"

"Perhaps he no longer thinks he does," answered Nuju. "We had best keep moving, before he saves the Matoran, builds the new koro, and awakens Mata Nui all by himself."

One by one, the Toa walked past the crystalline form of the Kranua. Matau was the last in line, and he stopped to gaze at the machine that had almost killed him. "I will tell you a dark secret," he whispered to the glass Vahki enforcer. "But only if you promise not to share."

Matau took a step to follow the others,

then turned around and gave the Kranua a gentle shove. It fell over and smashed into thousands of tiny fragments of crystal.

"Surrender and run aren't the only choices anymore," he said, walking away.

The tunnel widened as the Toa Metru marched on. The air grew warmer and more humid, which only seemed to quicken Vakama's pace. It was only when he reached what resembled a Matoran-made archway that he stopped.

Here the tunnel ceased to be enclosed for a distance, becoming instead a stone bridge over a chasm. Down below, scores of Rahi scuttled among the rocks, so many that it was almost impossible to see the ground beneath them.

"Scorpions," Vakama said to Nuju. "Thousands of them. I never imagined there were so many different species."

"And some of them are quite . . . unique," said the Toa of Ice. "The red-gold one on the far right ledge has three stingers. The black one fighting off his companions to the left has no legs.

Many of them are dead, though I can see no signs of violence on their bodies."

"I always forget about that telescopic lens in your mask," Vakama replied.

"I never do. Being able to see clearly is so important, don't you agree?"

Before Vakama could answer, Nuju was using his Mask of Telekinesis to lift a small specimen of the dead Rahi into the air. He deposited it on the bridge and knelt to examine it, while Vakama watched impatiently.

"I was right," Nuju said. "This creature didn't die in combat. It suffocated. It has no lungs, it has gills."

"You mean it's a sea creature? Then how . . . ?"

"I am not sure what it is, or what the rest of those beasts are," the Toa of Ice said, using his powers to lower the scorpion gently to a ledge. "And that troubles me."

Matau grimaced as he watched Vakama and Nuju inspecting a bug. *After all the hurry-rush, now they are blocking the path with an Onu-Matoran science project. Well, Mata Nui take this, I want to keep moving.*

The Toa of Air took off, flying over the heads of his two comrades and farther into the tunnels. He could hear Vakama behind him calling for him to come back, but ignored it. *The fire-spitter is getting a little too good at giving orders,* he said to himself.

It wasn't easy flying through a tunnel network. Worse, the twists and turns were coming much faster now. What had started out as a fairly straight course was rapidly turning into a maze, made navigable only by the presence of lightstones embedded in the stone walls. Matau landed to get his bearings. The last thing he wanted was to get lost a second time.

A wet sound came from his right, as if something was slithering across the ground. Matau unhooked his aero slicers from his back and set himself. He waited, still and silent, for the intruder to show itself.

When it did, the Toa of Air leapt backwards

as if scalded. Coiling before him was a serpent perhaps twenty feet long, with bright reddish skin and the head of a Rahkshi. Long, sharp horns curved up from the Rahi's brow. Behind it came other creatures, some crawling, some walking on two legs, others staggering as if about to drop from exhaustion.

The Rahkshi serpent hissed. Matau slowly backed away. He had no doubt he could win a fight against this beast, probably even most of its companions. But there were more coming up the tunnel every moment, with no end in sight, and Matau did not feel like battling an entire wing of the Archives.

He reached back to feel for the tunnel opening. The serpent's eyes caught the aero-slicer blade reflecting in the light. It reared back, energy crackling along the length of its horns and flowing from their tips to meet above the creature's head. A bolt flew from where the two streams joined, slamming Matau into the tunnel wall. Millions of volts surged through his body as he was forced back into the rock. Unconsciousness, when it came, was a mercy.

Nuju spotted the flash of light. "I believe Matau has found something."

"Or something has found him," said Onewa. "Do you think all Toa of Air blunder into things, or is it just him?"

"Let's find him," Vakama muttered, "so he can live and learn."

The five Toa broke into a run through the winding tunnel, Onewa in the lead. The Toa of Stone took a corner at high speed, only to smash into a Rahi Muaka coming the other way. The great cat barely took notice of the figure that struck it, which flew backwards from the impact. It simply growled a warning to anyone else that might be foolish enough to do the same thing that Onewa did.

None of the other Toa Metru were in a hurry to repeat Onewa's mistake. None of them had ever seen a Muaka quite like this in any

Archives exhibit. It wasn't just the extra sets of fangs or even the armor plating on its back and sides. No, it was more the hard protodermis thorns growing out of its legs, the ones gouging chunks out of the tunnel walls as it moved.

"Do you think Matau encountered this beast?" Nokama asked.

"If he did," replied Nuju, "I believe we may be short one Toa."

The Muaka lumbered forward, still ignoring the unconscious Onewa. It snarled at the Toa, but made no threatening moves. Vakama raised his hand, saying, "A burst of flame should confuse it, Nuju, and then you can ice it over."

"Wait a moment," broke in Nokama. "You may be the leader of this team, Vakama, but it is still a team."

"Is this really the time for a debate?"

"No," said the Toa of Water, taking a step toward the Rahi. "But it is a time for discussion."

Looking into the beast's eyes, Nokama gave a soft growl. The Muaka's eyes narrowed. It sniffed the air, then let out a deafening bellow. Nokama was unfazed, responding with a series of growls and snarls. Completely puzzled by this little creature speaking its language, the Muaka roared.

"He's in pain," Nokama said, not taking her eyes from the Rahi. "I can't . . . I can't get it clear, but I don't think he expected to find us. And I don't think he means us harm."

"Tell that to my head," said Onewa, slowly stirring. "How do we know he didn't hurt Matau? What are you suggesting, Nokama, that we pat him on the head and send him on his way?"

"Onewa has a point," offered Whenua. "If we let this Rahi pass, who is to say it will not take up residence on our new island home?"

Vakama frowned. Whenua was right, but a fight against this beast in a confined space would waste time, and that was assuming the Toa would win. If this Rahi made it to the island . . . well, that could be dealt with later.

"We let it go," he said. "Stand aside, brothers."

"What?" cried Onewa. "This thing flattens me, and we're just going to —"

The Muaka turned its head to look back at Onewa and gave a long, low growl. "I don't think he likes your attitude," Nokama chuckled.

The Rahi took a step forward, eyeing the Toa warily. When no one moved to stop his progress, he kept going, giving a final snarl as he went. All eyes turned to Nokama.

"What did he say?" asked Nuju.

"Two words," Nokama replied. "Turn back."

Vakama joined Whenua in the front of the group, using his flames to light the way so the Toa of Earth could take a rest. Nokama had helped Onewa to his feet, but the Toa of Stone insisted he needed no assistance to walk. Nuju brought up the rear, wondering if letting the Muaka pass was a decision they would regret in the future. Perhaps it truly represented no danger to the Toa, but who could know the mind of a Rahi?

They worked their way through the narrow, winding tunnels as swiftly as they dared. Whenua sensed no movement in the earth, but all that meant was that enemies could be waiting in ambush up ahead. Vakama was ready to hurl a spread of fireballs in a split second if an attacker appeared.

The Toa of Fire turned a corner and stopped, stunned. At first, he thought he had stumbled on some strange carving in the tunnel wall. But a closer examination revealed that this was no ancient work of art — it was the living form of Matau, somehow fused with the rock wall. The Toa of Air could not speak, but his eyes reached out to Vakama, pleading to be set free.

The other Toa were equally shocked. Matau had become part of the stone, with only a few inches of one aero-slicer blade and one hand still protruding from the wall. "Can't we just pull him out, somehow?" Nokama asked.

Onewa shook his head. "He is of the rock, and the rock is of him now. Pull him out by physical force and you would bring down the entire tunnel. No, this requires a more delicate approach. Vakama?"

The Toa of Fire focused his flames into as narrow a jet as possible. Then, slowly and carefully, he sliced through the rock around Matau. Whenua caught the slab as it came loose and gently lowered it to the ground.

Onewa knelt down and concentrated. In his time as a Toa Metru, he had used his elemental powers to achieve some amazing things. But never had the task been so difficult or the stakes been so high: a single slip, the slightest distraction, and it would mean Matau's life.

With unrelenting force of will, Onewa commanded the stone to reject that which did not belong. He could sense that the rock had interwoven with the substance of Matau and there would be no way to rip the Toa free. The rock would have to set him free. Painfully, inch by inch, he felt the stone retreat. Driven back by the power of the Toa Metru, it released its hold at last on Matau.

The Toa of Air gasped and scrambled to his feet. His mind reeled from the memories of being something else — not quite Toa, not quite stone, but some immobile hybrid of the two. He decided that he never again wanted to be anything but himself.

"What happened?" asked Onewa. "Who did this to you?"

"I will do better than speak-say," answered Matau. "I will show you while I make it pay."

It didn't take the Toa long to pick up the trail of the Rahi. Whenua could feel them moving along the tunnels. They had evidently turned the wrong way after attacking Matau and were headed deeper into the maze rather than toward the surface.

Nokama felt torn about the action they were about to undertake. True, the Rahi might have killed Matau. But she was convinced from talking with the Muaka that the beasts were acting out of panic, not rage. It might be that they needed the *help* of the Toa Metru.

Her foot caught on something and she almost stumbled. She looked down to see a clump of moss growing out of a crack in the floor. Now that she noticed it, there was moss all along the walls of this tunnel. She could not recall seeing any elsewhere on their journey. As a Matoran, she would have dismissed this as inconsequential. As a Toa, she had seen far too much to ignore anything out of the ordinary.

The tunnel forked. Whenua crouched down and tried to get a sense of which direction the Rahi had gone. He sensed traces of movement both to the right and the left, but nothing substantial.

"We go right," said Matau.

"Why?"

"Because I remember what happened the last time we went left," Matau replied.

They stumbled across the first dead Rahi about a quarter mile down the tunnel. It was a winged centipede about six feet long. Whenua didn't remember seeing anything like it in the Archives. A little more walking turned up a Rahkshi, a dozen ice bats, a lava eel that inexplicably had six legs, and a Kane-Ra bull that had none, all of them deceased.

Nuju and Whenua examined the bodies

one by one. Just as with the scorpion, there were no marks of violence. But unlike Nuju's past find, there was no obvious reason why these creatures should be dead.

"It almost seems as if they just . . . turned off," the Toa of Ice muttered. "But that makes no sense."

"Nothing else does," said Onewa. "Why should this be any different? Let's just hope whatever 'turned them off' doesn't decide to do the same to us."

Vakama signaled for the Toa to keep moving. They stepped carefully around the corpses, doing their best to stay focused on the task at hand. Perhaps that was why none of them noticed a portion of the slate gray tunnel wall detach, uncoil itself to its full length, and shift colors to the bright red of the Rahi serpent.

With the pale, dead eyes of a born hunter, it slithered after the Toa Metru.

Onewa cleared away some of the gray-green moss and inspected the walls of the tunnel. "Nokama, what do you make of this?"

The Toa of Water looked where he was pointing. A carving had been made in the wall, perhaps thousands of years ago judging by the Matoran dialect used and the erosion of the words. She focused the power of her Great Mask of Translation.

"It says Bohrok . . . and below, krana . . . and there's more," she reported, scraping away more of the moss. Strangely, the plant growth seemed to move aside just before she could tear it free from the wall. "Pictures. Two monstrous creatures, identical in size and shape, putting something into a pool — I cannot make out what — and drawing forth krana from its depths."

"You said that when we were sailing to the island, you spotted carvings on the walls beneath the water, didn't you?"

Nokama nodded. "I couldn't read them. The water had washed them away over time."

"These tunnels are not natural. Neither was the waterway leading from the Great Barrier to up above," said Onewa. "Someone dug them out of the stone, and I think I may know why. The Bohrok . . . what Vakama saw in his vision . . . these are the access tunnels for them to reach the surface."

"I thought you didn't believe in Vakama's vision," Nokama replied, smiling.

"Po-Matoran carvers don't believe in anything they cannot see, touch, and hit with a hammer," the Toa of Stone answered. "And if they do . . . they keep it to themselves."

"What do you think will be waiting for us in Metru Nui?" Whenua asked Vakama. It was a question that had been running through his mind for days. While he knew they had to return for the Matoran, he dreaded seeing what had become of his home.

"I don't know. With luck, the Matoran are still safe beneath the Coliseum. The power will be out and most of the chutes have probably collapsed. If the molten protodermis lines are ruptured, there is no telling what condition Ta-Metru is in. What about the Archives?"

"After the incident with Mavrah's Rahi years ago, they were reinforced to withstand shocks. But I am not sure the builders had such a massive quake in mind. If the Archive gates are down . . . if the stasis tubes within shattered . . ." Whenua looked at Vakama. His voice was grim. "Then there may not be a city to go back to."

Matau walked quickly and in uncharacteristic silence. Up to now, being a Toa had been fun, even when it seemed that danger was closing in from every side. After all, he was one of a select few beings who knew the thrill of adventuring and the satisfaction of saving an entire city. He had never seriously considered the possibility that he might get killed.

But in just the past few hours, he had twice confronted creatures that would have been more than happy to see him dead. It was a sobering reminder of what could happen to any of the Toa Metru, one that left him feeling as vulnerable as any Matoran.

The Toa of Air glanced at Nuju, who walked beside him. "I am sorry for being so mouth-closed."

"Actually, I was enjoying the change, but wondering about the reason for it," Nuju answered.

"I came close to being cold-dead. No more Toa-heroics, no more flying, no more fun . . . just the dark-sleep. Makes me think."

"Another change," murmured Nuju. "You're right, Matau. Any of us could be killed at any time. It's the risk of being a Toa. It's the price we pay for acting on our destiny, rather than allowing it to act on us. But don't forget one very important fact."

"What's that?"

Nuju clanked his fist against Matau's, so quickly that Matau thought he might have imagined it.

"You're still alive," said the Toa of Ice.

A whirl of lights and color. A sudden lurching feeling, as if the body was split apart from the spirit. Then a moment of crystal clarity, every detail of the surrounding area etched bright and clear as if bathed in sunlight.

Other senses returned quickly: the feel of stone beneath the feet; the sound of footsteps echoing in the distance; the acrid taste of hunger; and the scent . . . yes, the scent of the hated ones. The aroma of raw elemental power was so strong as to be almost overwhelming. The great beast did not know to where it had teleported, but it was certain now why it had been drawn to this spot.

There were Toa near. Heroes confident in their strength, secure in the rightness of their cause, and blissfully unaware of how little time they had left. The beast roared a challenge to its intended prey, a dire warning if they had the wits to perceive it:

The Rahi Nui was coming.

And it was coming to feed.

Whenua, linked to the earth as he was, first sensed the vibrations in the ground. It felt as if a thunderstorm was raging in the rock below their feet. Matau and Nokama, both attuned to nature in their own way, could hear the scratching and clawing of panicked Rahi scrambling to get out of the way of . . . something.

Then even the others, who had spent most of their lives focused on their work and not the world around them, could sense something was wrong. It was not a feeling they could put into words, rather the sensation that the universe had shifted somehow. A new element had been introduced, one that did not belong. Long before the sound of the Rahi Nui's footfalls reached them, all six Toa were ready for battle.

"This time, no long-wait," muttered Matau. "This time, cyclone first, questions later."

"And what if whatever is coming is friendly?" Nokama asked. Then she looked around. The others were staring at her as if she had just nominated Makuta to be a seventh Toa. She shrugged. "Well, the kikanalo were friendly," she added, under her breath.

"If one of us should be injured —" Nuju began.

"We keep fighting," Vakama said, cutting him off. "Retreat isn't an option. The Matoran are depending on us. No one should forget that."

"I hadn't," Nuju replied coldly. "I was going to say, if one of us is injured, I will make an ice barrier to shield them. It might afford a few moments of protection, at least. And it might help if you remember you are not the only Toa in the room, Vakama."

Vakama's reply was drowned out by the roar of the Rahi Nui. The Toa formed a ring, ready for anything — except, as it turned out, for the Rahi Nui to suddenly materialize behind them.

They whirled to see a monstrous creature towering over them, one that made the things they had already encountered look like the occupants of a Rahi petting zoo. Its head was that of a Kane-Ra bull, complete with razor-sharp horns. Its forearms were the powerfully muscled limbs of a Tarakava. The body and hind legs belonged to a great Muaka cat, and huge insectoid Nui-Rama wings sprouted from its shoulders. The nightmarish picture was made complete by the massive tail of a Nui-Jaga scorpion. So heavy was the Rahi Nui that the stone floor partially buckled beneath its feet. Every aspect of this horrible amalgamation felt like an offense to nature.

The Rahi Nui looked from one Toa to the next. In its long existence, the creature had rarely come across such a feast in the making. Six of the small ones, each practically aglow with energy, and each doomed to fall, as had so many before them.

When it reached Vakama, it paused. The beast could see defiance in the Toa's eyes, a most pleasing sight. The brave were always the most reckless, and their energies tasted so sweet.

Vakama was seeing something quite different when he looked at the Rahi Nui. Instead of seeing the face of a Kane-Ra, he saw the features of Nidhiki and Krekka superimposed on the monster. It took the Toa of Fire a moment to realize that this was another of his visions.

This beast is no simple Rahi, he said to himself. *It served the Dark Hunters. It hunted and killed at their command. There is no fear of Toa in its heart* — *to this creature, we are only prey.*

True to his word, Matau did not wait for the Rahi Nui to attack. Aiming his aero slicers, he sent twin cyclones at the beast. They struck with sufficient power to tear the Coliseum from its foundation and send it hurtling into the sea. But the Rahi Nui stood in the middle of the storm, unmoved.

The other Toa acted now. Fire, ice, water, stone, and earth rained down upon the Rahi Nui — to no effect. If anything, the creature seemed to be growing stronger. Through it all, the beast made no effort to defend itself or to stop the Toa Metru's attacks.

"Why is it just standing there?" wondered Nuju.

"Why shouldn't it?" answered Matau, bitterly. "We are doing nothing to pain-harm it."

"You're wrong, brother," said Nuju, grasping the truth at last. "Our attacks have been very effective . . . just not in the way we wanted. This isn't a fight for this monster — it's feeding time."

"What?" asked Vakama, as he signaled for the Toa to try and surround the beast.

"It isn't trying to stop us because we are giving it what it wants," Nuju continued. "Elemental energy. *Our* energy. It will soak up our powers until we are bone dry, given the opportunity."

There was wisdom in Nuju's words, Vakama knew. If this thing did feed on the powers of Toa, that would explain how it was able to hunt them. To the Rahi's trained senses, elemental energy had a scent that could be traced.

"Then we use mask powers," he said. "And let's hope it doesn't consider those dessert."

"I prefer the direct approach," said Onewa, ripping a jagged stone from the wall. He hurled it with all his might at the Rahi Nui and his aim was on the mark. The rock clipped the creature's leg, doing visible damage. The Rahi Nui roared in anger.

"There, see?" said the Toa of Stone, smiling. "When Toa powers don't work, try throwing a rock."

"You may want to look again," said Nokama. Onewa turned to see that the damage to the beast's leg was healing before his eyes. He had never seen the like before, except in Metru Nui when —

The revelation went off in his mind like an imploding force sphere. *Matoran work crews can make a damaged building "heal" that way, using Kanoka disks of regeneration,* he remembered. *And the way it appeared in our midst without any warning, almost as if it had . . . teleported.*

"Uh oh," said the Toa of Stone.

Vakama turned to him. "Did you just say 'uh oh'?"

"Yeah. I meant it, too," Onewa replied, keeping his voice low. "Load a disk. Pretend it's a powerhouse, and let our new friend know it."

Vakama nodded. He made a show of loading a disk into his launcher, saying, "The rest of you better shield your eyes and brace yourselves. There may not be much of the cavern left when this hits."

If the Rahi Nui did not understand the words, it did the tone. It snarled as Vakama took aim and fired. The disk flew on a straight course directly toward the spot between the beast's eyes, and then . . . the Rahi Nui was gone.

"That was some disk," said Matau, in wonder.

"That wasn't the disk, Matau," said Onewa, his eyes scanning the stone floor. "It wasn't a teleport either. Our Rahi didn't want to stay around to see what was in that disk, so it shrank out of the way."

"Shrank?" repeated Whenua. "Something that size . . . it's not possible . . . without a Kanoka disk to . . ." Then the answer came to him as well.

"The disks! Mata Nui, it has the powers of the disks!"

"Then it may well be unstoppable," Vakama said. "Prepare, brothers and sister, for what may be our final battle."

"And happy-cheer is here again," added Matau, meaning not a word of it.

5

The Toa Metru waited in silence. They knew the monster was still in the cavern with them, too small to see, and could strike at any moment. Whenua had suggested that Nuju simply freeze over the floor, but was reminded that the beast fed on elemental energies.

"Perhaps we should seek a narrower tunnel, where its bulk will work against it," suggested Nokama.

"A good thought, sister," agreed Onewa. "But then we would be unable to attack it together."

"And some of us need room to quick-move," said Matau, smiling. "Maybe I can dazzle it with my style — after all, it worked on you, Nokama."

"I think we need to get you back above

ground," the Toa of Water replied. "Your brain has frozen."

The attack, when it came, was too sudden and swift to be defended against. The Rahi Nui shot back up to full size in the midst of the Toa, sending them flying. Whenua was the first to try to rise, only to be smashed almost into unconsciousness by the Rahi Nui's powerful forearm.

Matau mentally triggered his aero slicers, taking off with the intention of mounting an assault from the air. Seeing the creature moving to finish off Whenua, he dove. But the Rahi Nui's move had been a ruse to draw the Toa of Air in closer. As soon as he was near, the beast jerked its head and caught Matau on its horns. Then another sudden movement sent the Toa crashing to the hard ground.

Barely fighting a few seconds and we've lost a third of our number, thought Vakama. In front of him, Nokama used her hydro blades to fend off the beast's blows. Onewa and Nuju were attempting to scale opposite sides of the Rahi Nui, hanging on despite the creature's efforts to shake them off.

The Toa of Fire launched a flame blast at the ceiling above the beast's head. His fires melted through the stone, bringing a rain of red-hot magma down on the Rahi. Enraged, the beast roared and abruptly grew in size. Nuju managed to jump clear and use an ice slide to reach the ground, but Onewa had almost reached the back of the Rahi. The sudden growth caught him by surprise and he was flung from the monster to plunge to the cavern floor far below.

Nokama spotted the danger and broke into a run. She knew she would have to time her leap perfectly, or both she and Onewa were going to wind up nothing but shattered pieces. At just the right moment, she used her powerful legs to launch herself into the air. She caught the falling Onewa in mid-leap, then hurled a blast of water at the floor. The jet of water acted as a brake, lowering them gently to the ground.

"Next time, hang on tighter," Nokama said

gently. "Or fall closer to Nuju, he would love tossing some ice your way."

Onewa's eyes widened. "Nokama, look out!"

The Toa of Stone shoved her hard, but too late. The Rahi Nui's stinger slammed into Nokama and buried itself in the armor of her back. Onewa's power surged from him, causing a stone vise to come forth from the floor and grip the monster's tail. Angered, the Rahi yanked hard to free itself, smashing the rock and at the same time releasing Nokama.

The Toa of Water pitched forward. Onewa caught her before she could hit the ground. Her eyes were dark and her heartlight was flashing erratically. She was barely breathing as Onewa laid her down.

Onewa lifted his eyes, rage filling his heart. He triggered his mask power, but not to try to control the Rahi Nui. No, this time he sent his mental energies like a lance into the monster's brain. *What I can control, I can destroy,* the Toa of Stone thought darkly.

The Rahi Nui paused, feeling something strange coming over it. Then a pain more intense than anything it had ever known exploded in its mind. The beast bellowed and staggered as the power of the Mask of Mind Control tore through its thoughts.

"I don't know what you are, or what you have done before," Onewa snarled. "But you have never faced anything like me. Feel my power and fall!"

And, indeed, it looked as if that was about to happen. This attack was not something the Rahi Nui could defend against, and it reeled as Onewa increased the pressure, shrinking back to its normal size. But the beast had very little mind to blast, and after what seemed like forever, it suddenly realized the horrible pain would not get any worse. The creature drew strength from that thought. Forcing itself to ignore the blistering attack, the Rahi Nui charged.

Focused completely on tapping the mask's powers, Onewa could not get out of the way in time. The horned head of the Rahi Nui smashed the Toa of Stone into the wall and sent him down into darkness.

Now only Vakama and Nuju stood against the beast. Ordinarily, there was little that fire and ice could not accomplish when they worked together. But against a creature that could so easily demolish four Toa, what chance did they have?

Vakama turned to see that Nuju had evidently cracked under the strain. With the menace of a massive Rahi looming over them, the Toa of Ice was busy examining the creature's footprints in the shattered stone.

"Nuju!" he shouted. "You're not in a Knowledge Tower now! Stop analyzing and start fighting!"

"I think I have the key," the Toa of Ice said. "Buy me time!"

Vakama threw up a wall of flame, cutting the Rahi Nui off for a moment. Then he raced over to Nuju, still half-convinced the Toa of Ice had simply lost his mind. "What key?"

"Look at these," said Nuju. "This footprint is from the monster at normal size . . . this one from when he grew larger. There's something very curious about the differences between them."

The Toa of Fire glanced at both. He still didn't see what Nuju was talking about. "There are no differences. They're identical."

"That is what's very curious," Nuju replied, rising. "There *should* be a difference."

Beams shot out from the Rahi Nui's eyes, freezing the wall of flame. Then a single blow smashed it into icy shards. But the barrier had done its job, and Nuju's words had sparked an idea in Vakama's mind. Perhaps there was a way to defeat this creature, after all . . .

"We need to make him grow, and I know how," said the Toa of Fire. He attached his disk launcher to his back, preparing to use it as a rocket pack.

Nuju shook his head. "You saw what happened to Matau. That thing will swat you like a fireflyer."

"Not if I get high enough, fast enough. What other choice do we have?"

Nuju had to admit that there was none that he could see. Without another word, Vakama activated the launcher and soared into the air. The beast swiped at him as he flew by, but missed. Once Vakama had reached a high enough altitude so as to be out of the creature's reach, he began tossing fireballs that burst in midair.

Below him, the Rahi Nui grew angry. It was impatient to finish off these last two small ones and feast upon their elemental energies. But this one persisted in buzzing about and filling the air with bright light and heat. Although the Toa-created flames were in fact food for the creature, in its dim mind it still had the instinctive dislike of fire common to most Rahi. Again and again, it lashed out, only to have Vakama dodge its blows.

On the ground, Nuju waited impatiently. He had grasped Vakama's plan — it was the only course of action that made sense, now that he thought about it — but it depended on the reactions of the beast. *If the beast is too simpleminded to realize the best way to stop a flying foe,* he thought. *Or if Vakama should fly too close . . .*

Nuju thought he glimpsed a change, if a small one. Activating the telescopic lens in his mask, he focused on the Rahi Nui. Yes, it had begun to grow, but slowly. He wondered if the combat with the Toa had begun to tax its energies.

Well, we cannot have that, can we? the Toa of Ice thought to himself, readying his crystal spikes.

High above, Vakama had spotted the monster's size increasing as well. He gave a signal to Nuju, then launched twin streams of fire from his outstretched hands. At the same time, Nuju hurled ice blast after ice blast at the massive creature. As Vakama expected, this had the same effect as tossing a torch into a Ta-Metru fire pit: It added to the Rahi Nui's already considerable power. Practically glowing with raw energy, the beast continued to grow larger and larger.

The Toa of Fire narrowly evaded another blow. The monster was easily half the size of the Coliseum now, and its growth rate showed no sign of stopping. For a moment, he wondered if he had been wrong in his guess about the beast's nature.

If I am, I won't live to regret it, he knew. *One blow from that massive arm and I'll be shattered into shards.*

Caught up in his questions, Vakama never saw the Rahi Nui's next attack. Moving incredibly fast, its tail stinger slashed through the air, aiming directly for Vakama's chest. Too late, the Toa spotted the danger and tried to jet out of the way. The stinger descended, death just inches away . . . it struck . . . Vakama waited for the pain and the darkness.

But he felt nothing. The Rahi Nui's stinger had passed through his body as if its owner were a ghost. The beast, still growing, looked confused. It struck again and again with its powerful arms, only to find itself unable to make contact. Vakama could see the creature's form wavering like a heat mirage. It roared, but the sound was a hollow one.

Vakama dove as the creature continued to grow and its form grew less and less distinct. Now its head and shoulders had disappeared from view, passing through the ceiling of the cave. The two Toa continued to pour elemental energy into the Rahi Nui, even as it grew larger still and faded from view. With a final, mournful wail, the beast was gone, disappearing as if it had never existed.

Nuju cut off his ice blasts and dropped to the ground, exhausted. "Let's . . . not . . . do that again," he said, making an effort to catch his breath.

"But it worked," Vakama replied. "You were right, the footprints were the key."

Nuju ran his hand along the outline of one of the huge imprints the creature had left in the stone. "Increased size without increased weight. Its body was expanding, but not its total mass. So when we made it grow, and then fed it even more power . . ."

"Its growth outraced its mass," said Vakama. "It eventually got too big to retain any density, and its atoms drifted apart."

Nuju glanced around at the damage done to the cave. "Let us hope it takes a long, long time to pull itself together. A thousand years would be just about right."

Behind them, Matau and Whenua had made it back to their feet. In a corner, Onewa had awakened also and was trying to rouse Nokama. Nuju didn't need his enhanced vision to see that something was very wrong with the Toa Metru of Water.

Onewa looked up at his friends, panic in his eyes. "She's dying . . . Nokama's dying!"

6

Whenua looked down at the still form of Nokama. The spark of life was barely present in her. He had no doubt it was only her strong will that was keeping her clinging to existence. "We have to turn back," he said. "If we return to the island, we can at least make her comfortable before . . ."

"He's right," said Onewa. "These tunnels are full of dangers. We can't risk further harm to her."

Matau scooped up Nokama in his arms. Onewa and Whenua had already started walking back the way they had come and now Matau fell in line behind them. They didn't look back, assuming that Vakama and Nuju would be following.

"We're not going back," said Vakama. "Neither are you. We keep on for Metru Nui, all of us."

Shocked, Onewa whirled on Vakama. He was even more surprised to see Nuju standing with the Toa of Fire, his silence saying he agreed with this ridiculous statement. What was wrong with them?

"And then what?" demanded Onewa. "Even if we make it back, even if Nokama doesn't die on the way, there is no one there to help her! The city is in ruins. The Matoran are locked in Makuta sleep."

"Exactly," replied Vakama. "Hundreds of Matoran have had their lives stolen from them. They are depending on us to save them. That has to be more important than any one life, even Nokama's. I'm sorry."

Onewa unlimbered his proto pitons and started for Vakama. "Not as sorry as you're going to be, fire-spitter!"

Nuju stepped in between the two Toa. The look in his eyes said it would not be wise to challenge him. "Stop it now. It is an insult to Nokama for us to stand here arguing while her life slips away. Onewa, returning to the island is condemning her to death, for there is nothing there that can cure her."

The Toa of Ice turned to Vakama. "And you should remember that there are better reasons to return to Metru Nui than just our mission. There may be ancient lore in the Knowledge Towers that could save Nokama."

"If we are going down-side, we had better go," said Matau. "She is growing worse."

The Toa headed out of the cave in an uncomfortable silence. Whenua offered to carry Nokama, but Matau shook him off. "I will keep my Toa-friend safe," he vowed.

They moved at a much faster pace now, ignoring carvings on the walls or side tunnels. Onewa stayed close to Matau, as if he thought his proximity might somehow keep Nokama's heartlight flashing that much longer.

The tunnels grew narrower as they descended and the moss covering the stone seemed to be everywhere. Onewa's shoulder brushed against a clump and it clung to his armor. He brushed it off, disgusted, saying, "What is this stuff?"

"I've never seen anything like it in the mines," Whenua answered, reaching out to examine some. To his surprise, it moved to avoid his touch. "Now that's strange."

"Can we not think-worry about plants?" snapped Matau. "Our Toa-sister needs us."

The Toa of Air went to take another step, only to find that his foot would not move. He looked down and saw that hundreds of tiny vines had sprung from the stone floor and wrapped themselves around his ankles. All of the other Toa were similarly afflicted. Vakama sent a narrow stream of fire to burn off the vines. As soon as flame touched his bindings, a thicker, thorned vine shot out from the wall and wrapped itself around his throat, choking him.

Vakama seized hold of the vine, struggling to get it off him. But it took the help of Nuju to overcome its strength and tear it loose. Vakama gasped, filled with dread at the thought that an old enemy might have returned.

"Morbuzakh . . ." he whispered.

The voice that answered him came from

everywhere at once, sounding like the snapping of dead branches. It was not the sibilant hiss of the Morbuzakh, but was heavy with the same feeling of corruption and decay.

"No," it said. "I am what the Morbuzakh wished it could be."

Nuju unleashed his ice power, covering one wall of moss in a thick frost. Harsh laughter filled the tunnel. An instant later the ice shattered like glass. "I am not that weakling, Nuju. Oh, yes, I know who you are. I know all my enemies."

Onewa succeeded in wrenching one leg free. "Enemies? We have never encountered you before. And before you set yourself against us, you might want to think about how the Morbuzakh wound up: ash in the wind."

Vines like tentacles snaked down the tunnel toward them. One by one, they wrapped themselves around the Toa Metru, pulling them free and dragging them deeper into the darkness. Matau protested as a vine grabbed Nokama out of his arms and carried her unconscious form away.

"Come to me," said the voice. "Come and learn why I hate you beyond all other beings, save one. Come and learn how you have wronged me, and how you shall pay."

Matoran legend speaks of a time long, long before the founding of Metru Nui, perhaps even before the coming of the Great Spirit Mata Nui himself. In those ancient times, Matoran labored ceaselessly and in darkness, little knowing the reasons for the work they did. Those Matoran who did their jobs well would be rewarded by being allowed to journey to a place called Artakha, where they could work in the light and with no fears about their future. In time, Artakha became known in myth as the "Great Refuge" where all Matoran would be safe from harm.

But life was very different for those Matoran who worked poorly. They were consigned to a place that made the Ta-Metru Great Furnace look like a minor heat source. No one knew what happened there, but it was said that no Matoran who went to that place ever returned. This frightening location never had a name of its own, but was instead referred to by the name of the being who ruled it:

"Karzahni," a voice whispered.

Vakama was startled to hear that dreaded name spoken by the plant creature that held him prisoner. But he had to admit that the cavern to which he had been brought might well have been a home to that figure of myth. While there were no flames to be seen, the cave was littered with mutant Rahi, some dying, some very much alive. But he sensed it was not death that ruled here — it was fear, so overwhelming as to be almost toxic.

The plant itself looked little like the Morbuzakh. It was less a creature of vines than of twisted trunk and branches, resembling a warped, mangled version of one of the trees on the island above. Its substance was interlaced with the rock of the cave, even more so than the Morbuzakh's had been with the Great Furnace.

"You know the name," the creature whispered. "Of course you do. It amused my creator to give me the name of a being so hated and feared by Matoran past . . . as if somehow that power to evoke dread would then live on in me."

"What do you want of us?" asked Nuju.

"Want? I want nothing," the Karzahni replied. "Petty desires are for lesser beings. But need? Ah, there is much that I need, and much that you can provide. And to start, a gift . . ."

The Toa's eyes followed one of the vines, as it moved slowly toward a far wall. Pinned against the rock was a form Matau recognized all too well: the huge serpent that had attacked him in the tunnels.

"A friend of yours, I believe," said the Karzahni. "I found him snaking through the passages, no doubt planning to strike at you again. The foolish creature thought he could escape my notice."

The Karzahni's voice dropped lower. Its tone suggested he was talking with trusted co-conspirators. "That is why his kind will not survive, Toa . . . and mine will rule."

A half-rotted branch gestured toward the

other Rahi that slithered, crawled, and staggered through the cave. "My needs are simple: power and revenge. Power I have, over such as these — failed experiments of my creator. But revenge . . . that you cheated me of, Toa Metru, and so my vengeance shall fall upon you."

"What is he talking about?" Onewa whispered to Nuju.

"I don't know," replied the Toa of Ice. "But if there is one thing we learned from the Morbuzakh, it is that it is useless to argue with vegetation."

"Wouldn't your revenge be sweeter against all six of us?" Vakama asked their captor. "How can you take the full measure of satisfaction from it when one of our number is dying?"

"We are all dying here, Toa," the Karzahni said, as calmly as if he were discussing the weather. "I simply intend to make sure that I die last."

The vines released the six Toa, even laying Nokama gently on the cavern floor. Matau knelt to check her condition, but it had only grown worse in the time since their capture. "What trouble-harm have we caused you, monster, that you keep us from saving our friend?" demanded the Toa of Air.

"You have robbed from me, Matau," came the answer. "You attacked my creator, imprisoned him in a place I cannot reach, and for that you must atone."

Of course, thought Vakama. *Why didn't we see it before?* "Makuta," he breathed. "Makuta created you and we defeated him. Now you're angry because you want to rescue your creator."

"Rescue? *Rescue?*" The Karzahni's laughter became a deafening shriek. "Fools! I want Makuta dead!"

The Toa stood in stunned silence, hardly able to believe what they had just heard. For a long time, no one spoke. Then Whenua's curiosity could not be contained anymore. "If Makuta created you," he began, "then why . . . ?"

"Created me . . . and rejected me," rumbled the Karzahni. "He made me too well. I am too powerful and too wise. I would not have been content to drive the inhabitants from the outskirts of the city, or even to rule Metru Nui. I would have brought down the places of the Matoran, all of them, and ended their reign! I did not want their obedience or their loyalty, as Makuta did — only their destruction."

Vakama could think of nothing to say. All of this fit with theories he had formed during the journey to the island, but now it had all been confirmed. Makuta had created the Morbuzakh and unleashed it on Metru Nui, as a prelude to his plan to doom all the Matoran to centuries of sleep. The Karzahni had been his first attempt, but it was too powerful for Makuta's purposes.

But where he failed to defeat us, thought the Toa of Fire, *this thing just might succeed.*

Nokama moaned. The Karzahni's branches moved toward her, but Matau slapped them away with his aero slicers. For a moment, it seemed as if the branches would attack, but instead they slowly lowered to the ground.

"Your friend has little time left," the

Karzahni said. "And as Vakama suggested, I have need of all six of you, though for reasons he cannot suspect. I can heal her, temporarily. Then you will do a task for me. Succeed, and I might be persuaded to cure the Toa of Water's affliction."

Onewa glanced at Nuju, then at Vakama. It was obvious that none of them believed the Karzahni for a moment. But if Nokama were to be restored to health, even for a brief time, they would at least have a fighting chance. And that was all Toa ever needed.

One of the branches moved anew. Matau went to defend her again, but Vakama shook his head. The Toa of Air stepped aside, never taking his eyes off the arm of the plant. It hovered over Nokama and then twisted itself again and again, finally squeezing a few drops of thick, silvery liquid from itself. They fell into Nokama's mouth. In a matter of moments, light returned to her eyes.

"Where am I? What . . . ?" she said, sitting up.

Matau reached out to give her a hug. Nokama pushed him away, saying, "Have you gone crazy, brother? And what is that . . . that thing? Where is the great beast we were fighting?"

"Same day, different monster," said the Toa of Air, helping her to her feet.

Vakama took a step forward. "And what is this task, then?"

"A simple one, for such brave heroes," the Karzahni answered, mockingly. "You six will take the south passage from this cave. Along the way, you will find a vault set in the wall of the tunnel. From that you will take a black vial. You will use that vial to collect a sample of energized proto-dermis from one of Makuta's many lairs and bring it back here to me."

"If it's so simple, why don't you do it?" asked Onewa.

The Karzahni's branches rustled in annoy-ance. "I am not built for mobility — this you would see, Toa of Stone, were your head not filled with rocks as well."

Onewa ignored the insult and looked at the cave with a tactician's eye. He had little doubt that the Toa Metru assembled could fight this creature and win. But then what? If it crumbled as the Morbuzakh had, then there would be no way to get more of the antidote for Nokama. Hard as it was for him to admit, they did not need a battle right now, they needed time to think.

Vakama evidently agreed, for he said, "All right, Karzahni. We will do your errand. But if you plan any treachery —"

"Oh, come now," replied the Karzahni. "The false Turaga Dume . . . the Vahki . . . Ahkmou . . . even Makuta himself — you of all beings should understand, Vakama. What is life without a little treachery?"

7

When Whenua first went to work in the Onu-Metru Archives, he made a classic beginner's mistake: He got lost. He had been sent to the fourth sublevel to check on an ash bear exhibit, but lost count and wound up two levels down. Unknown to him, this area had been used by Mavrah for an experiment with Kinloka rodents some time back, but the rodents had broken free and the level had been quarantined. Over time, the Kinloka had eaten the barriers and the lightstones and it was only their instinctive fear of the Nui-Rama on the level above that kept them from rampaging throughout the Archives.

Even now, he could remember walking through the dark and deserted wing, hearing the Kinloka skittering all around him. Now and then, one or two would rush up and snap at him, then dash away. It had been bad when he wasn't sure what was down there with him — and worse when he realized, because everyone knew Kinloka would eat *anything* that didn't eat them first. Every instinct in Whenua told him to run as fast as he could, but his mind told him that was the best way to end up lost forever.

Walking through the south tunnel brought back those memories in full force. As unscientific as it seemed to a veteran archivist, the atmosphere of these tunnels felt evil. Even if he ignored the carvings of bizarre Rahi and the twisted creatures that crawled and flew past him, he could not escape the fact that monstrous things had been done in this place. The sooner they were away from here and back in Metru Nui, the happier he would be. After all, even quake-damaged, the city *had* to be better than this.

Vakama was directly behind Whenua, but kept stopping to pick up the Kanoka disks that littered the passage. Their appearance here had been a mystery until he spotted a broken vault containing a few disks and carvings of Kanohi masks unlike any he had seen before. Evidently, Makuta had been dabbling in mask making, but with what success it was impossible to tell.

Onewa had the hard job on the journey. Using his connection to stone, he was attempting to sense hollow spaces in the walls that might house the vault they were looking for. Nokama was sticking close to him, if only to escape Matau, who had been hovering over her since her return to consciousness.

"Are you getting anything?" she asked, for the fourth time in as many minutes.

"I'm not sure. There's something just ahead here, but it doesn't feel like . . . wait." Onewa ran his hands slowly over a section of the wall. "Behind here. I don't know what's inside, but it's definitely a compartment of some kind."

The other Toa crowded around. Whenua offered to use his drills to open the vault, but Onewa turned him down. "This way is more fun," he said, rearing back to punch a hole in the wall.

Toa fist met stone, and stone lost. The heroes struggled to see the contents of the chamber through the cloud of rock dust. Impatient, Onewa leaned forward. "I think I spotted something."

A shape shot from the inside of the chamber, so fast it was just a blur. Then Onewa staggered backwards, hands to his mask, screaming, "Get it off!"

Nokama rushed to him. There was something clinging to his Kanohi, but she had never seen its like before. It had the ridged features of Bohrok krana she had seen in the Archives, and the longer, serpentine shape of a Rahkshi kraata. But there was no time to analyze it, for she could already see the effect it was having on the Toa of Stone.

Onewa's arms had dropped to his sides. When he spoke, his voice had become mechanical, the way Nokama imagined a Vahki might speak if its programming allowed it to do so. "They . . . they . . . they . . ." he repeated, again and again.

Whenua moved to tear the creature off of Onewa's Kanohi, but Nuju blocked him. "Wait. Let him talk," said the Toa of Ice. "We may learn something of value. Onewa, 'they' who? Who are you talking about?"

The Toa of Stone turned slowly to look at Nuju. His eyes were vacant. "They . . . too late . . . too late for anything . . . all must end. Visorak. Visorak." Onewa began to tremble violently. "Visorak! The end! They wait. They watch. They know. They . . . they know . . ."

"Nuju, stop this!" cried Nokama.

Vakama stepped forward. "To blazes with knowledge, this is one of us," he said, launching a firebolt. The flames consumed the creature, reducing it foul-smelling ash. So precise was Vakama's control that Onewa's mask was not even singed. The Toa of Stone staggered backwards, reaching back to the wall to keep from falling.

"Are you all right?" asked Nokama.

"Yes . . . I will be . . ." he replied, badly shaken. "But . . . I would not wish that experience on anyone else."

"What did you see? What are Visorak?" Nuju pressed.

Onewa shook his head, confused. "I don't know. Those were not my words, not my thoughts. I remember . . . something . . . something horrible, everywhere . . . stealers of life . . . but I cannot see more. Vakama? Is this what your visions are like?"

The Toa of Fire, shrugged, uncomfortable at the question. He had never grown used to his erratic visions of the future. "I suppose so. Sometimes."

"Then I pity you, brother," Onewa said softly. "I truly do."

Whenua had turned his attention back to the vault. If anyone had asked, he was simply searching for the vial they were here to find. But secretly, he half-hoped there might be a second one of those creatures inside. *What a Rahi for study,* he thought. *A hybrid, perhaps, and a symbiote . . . I would stake my reputation on it. Nuju was right, we could have learned so much — but not at the risk of Onewa's sanity.*

To his disappointment, there was nothing

else alive in the vault. But nestled in the back there was a vial made of a peculiar, black metallic substance. Whenua grabbed it and turned to the other Toa, "We have begun. Now we only need the energized protodermis."

Matau smiled. "Librarian, that is like saying we 'only' need to clean-polish a Muaka's teeth . . . from the inside."

After all they had been through on the journey thus far, the Toa Metru hoped for an uneventful passage to Makuta's lair. They were badly disappointed. The closer they came to their destination, the thicker and faster came the Rahi, both creatures they were familiar with and mutants not even a mad Matoran could have dreamed of. Some fled, and some fought, but the Toa found no glory in the battles. Even Nuju, who had never encouraged any connection between himself and the natural world, could sense that these beasts attacked out of desperation, not evil. The realization chilled even the Toa of Ice.

It might have been after their tenth victory, or their hundredth, that Nuju gave voice to his thoughts. They had all lost count of how many Rahi they had defeated, and dreaded the new waves that were sure to come. Matau had looked around at the scene of the struggle, saying, "Even trapped, Makuta has many guard-fighters. He must need his alone-time when he is making monsters."

"They aren't guards," Nuju said. "Maybe they were at one time, but they aren't trying to stop us from reaching our destination."

"Then why all the slash and roar?"

"It's not so strange, Matau. How would you react if you were trying to escape someplace, and others blocked your way?"

Nuju's words stopped Vakama in his tracks. He grasped their implications immediately, and wished he could just dismiss the Toa of Ice's theories as nothing more than dark fantasies springing from this terrible place. The only problem was Nuju had a nasty habit of being right.

"Think about it," the Toa of Ice continued.

"The Nui-Jaga who ran to its death . . . the Muaka whose pain Nokama sensed . . . and the strange creatures we have encountered all along this journey. We have grown so used to battle that we see enemies even when there are none, brothers and sister. These beasts are not charging toward us — they are running away from something."

"Do you remember the stone rat plague?" asked Whenua. "You know, when they swarmed up out of the streets of Ta-Metru and devastated the district for weeks? Everyone thought it was hunger and instinct that drove them to the surface . . . until we discovered the Nui-Rama swarm loose in the maintenance tunnels, preying on the rats' nests."

Vakama's memories of that terrible time were all too vivid. Even Toa Lhikan, who had defeated the mightiest Rahi, almost found himself helpless before an assault by some of the smallest. "They hadn't mounted an attack on the metru," he remembered aloud. "They were just trying to get away from something worse than themselves."

The Toa stood in silence, thinking about the scores of monstrosities they had faced since entering this maze of shadows. And the same question echoed in all their minds: *What could possibly be more terrible than what we have seen?*

There were no carvings to point the way to Makuta's lair, no signs warning the Toa to go back if they valued their lives. Only darkness greeted them as they descended ever deeper — darkness and the incessant whisper of the Karzahni, speaking through the plant growth on the tunnel walls.

"Now, Toa," it said urgently. "You draw closer to my birthplace. Already you can feel your spirits grow cold and your minds rebel. This place is alive with memories, twisted memories of madness. Tread carefully, my allies."

"Allies," muttered Vakama. "I would sooner team with Makuta himself."

"Makuta is not here," whispered the Karzahni. "And I am. It is truly a circumstance ripe with possibilities."

The argument was ended by Whenua, who

stood before a dead end in the tunnel. "I think we have found it, Vakama. But I can feel something in the ground . . . a power . . . movement. Something is in there, I'm sure of it."

"Then let's not keep it waiting," said Vakama. Placing his hand on the metallic gateway, he melted a hole through its substance. Then he stepped aside to allow Whenua to reach inside and grab hold. With a great heave, the Toa of Earth tore the door from its hinges.

The smell of smoke, rot, and molten protodermis struck the Toa Metru like a fist. They half expected to see the winged, armored shape of their nemesis emerge from the darkness within, but nothing moved beyond the entryway. Hesitantly, the Toa stepped into the chamber, every sense alert for danger.

Massive stone pillars stood in the four corners of the lair, carved with symbols so ancient even Nokama's Mask of Translation proved useless. The walls were lined with large stasis tubes, much like the ones used in the Archives. Some were shattered, others still housed Rahi, most of them dead. The creatures were altered beyond all recognition, and in some cases, it seemed impossible that they could ever have existed.

The dominant feature of the chamber was a huge, silvery pool of energized protodermis in the center of the floor. Its surface was so calm that Nuju almost thought it might be a sheet of ice. The Toa Metru gathered around the circular pit that held the object of Karzahni's desire.

"Imagine," Matau said. "If this can do what Nuju speak-says . . ."

"The power to create, and to destroy," Nuju whispered. "What could be greater? With this, one could be elevated to heights undreamed of."

"Or be doomed to the darkness below," said Vakama. "Let's not forget that the Morbuzakh, the Karzahni, and a legion of monsters were spawned in this place, born of Makuta's madness and power like this."

The Toa of Fire took the vial from Whenua and knelt down to take a sample from the pool. "The sooner we have what we seek and get away from here, the better I will like it."

At the slightest touch of the vial, the energized protodermis began to boil. Matau pulled
Vakama away from the edge as the liquid grew
more agitated, as if building to an explosion.
Then, before the startled eyes of the Toa Metru,
something rose from the pool.

At first, they thought it was simply a wave
of protodermis that would engulf them. But the
liquid hung suspended and then began to reshape
itself, forming a head and two arms. Features began to appear on the face and hands to grow
from the ends of the limbs. Yet, through it all, the
substance never changed, only the shape, as it
took on the semblance of the Toa Metru. When
all was done, what hovered above the pool was a
living entity made entirely of energized protodermis.

"I am the guardian of this place," it said.
Though its tone was calm and emotionless, its
voice rumbled like thunder in the chamber. "You
have come to take that which is forbidden. It is
not to be."

"Who are you to deny us?" asked Vakama

boldly. "We are Toa Metru from the city of legends, seeking only a small portion of what you protect for a vital mission."

"Do you seek to create, or to undo creation?" asked the protodermis being.

"Neither," said Nuju. "We are attempting to buy safe passage to Metru Nui from the Karzahni, with hopes of saving the Matoran trapped in eternal sleep in that place."

A ripple ran through the being as it pondered Nuju's words. Then it fixed its eyes upon the Toa of Ice and said, "The Karzahni is known to me, for I was there at its birth . . . a pretender to the throne of shadows, it was, from its first moment of existence. I have no love for it, yet still you may not have what you seek."

"But the Matoran —"

"What are the Matoran to me?" snapped the entity. "They are but the living. I am life. Behold."

The being raised an arm and a stream of energized protodermis flowed from its hand. It struck a tiny buzzing insect that flew near the ceiling. The Toa watched in awe as the insect metamorphosized, growing to a thousand times its original size, its wingspan easily 200 feet across, its stinger replaced by a jaw filled with metallic teeth. It dove at the assembled Toa Metru.

"Scatter!" shouted Vakama. "Together we are too easy a target!"

Nuju aimed an ice bolt at the flying monstrosity. The creature responded by flapping its wings so fast they became a blur. The ice projectile stopped just short of the beast and rebounded toward Nuju, striking the Toa of Ice squarely and knocking him off his feet.

"Interesting," murmured the protodermis entity. "Its defense mechanisms have been enhanced, so that wing vibration generates a field capable of reflecting back force hurled against it."

"This isn't some experiment!" Whenua shouted, narrowly avoiding another pass by the mutated insect. "This is real!"

"As real as the Metru Nui Archives?" replied the entity. "Did you worry about the feelings of the lesser beings you caged and studied and gawked at? No, Toa. I am as far beyond you as you are from the lowliest Rahi. You are all insects to me."

Onewa backflipped out of the way of the monster's snapping jaws. "Great. We're getting battered and he's giving lectures."

As the other Toa fought a holding action against the entity's creation, Nokama stood to the side and studied its movements. Although now far more dangerous, the beast's instincts had not changed, and nor had its strategies. Instead of charging and demolishing its foes, it persisted in diving and then retreating, as a small insect would. She saw an opening, and knew that there was no one better to take advantage of it than her — after all, her hours were numbered regardless.

When the creature dove again, she jumped on its back. It immediately climbed toward the ceiling, but she hung on, inching her way up toward its head. Positioned as she was, the beast could not turn to snap at her, but it swooped and dove in an effort to shake her off.

Nokama readied her hydro blade. Before the beast could react, she had slipped the tool across its neck and then grabbed it with her other hand. Then she pulled hard on the blade, back and to the right. Faced with the prospect of turning or choking, the creature veered to the right.

"What is that crazy teacher doing?" asked Onewa.

"Steering," replied Nuju.

"I wonder if that would work with Gukko birds?" wondered Matau.

High above, Nokama was engaged in a war of wills with the creature. Every time it tried to dive toward the Toa Metru, she yanked hard and forced it back up. It made a noise that was a combination of a buzz and a screech. Using the Mask of Translation, Nokama replied, "I am not letting go. You can crash into a wall and kill us both, or you can work with me."

Nokama's fellow Toa watched as the creature slowly went from flying wildly and erratically to circling near the cavern ceiling. Even having previously seen Nokama engage in conversation with a Kikanalo herd chief, they found it hard to believe she could tame such a beast. The protodermis entity had watched her efforts with interest as well, but the expression on his liquid features indicated he had lost patience with the display.

"What I begin," he said, raising his arm, "I can also end." A jet of energized protodermis flew from him to strike the airborne creature. It writhed at the touch of the fluid and plummeted to the ground. Nokama leapt from its back and used blasts of water to slow her descent until Matau could safely catch her.

The Rahi hit the ground and lay still, before finally dissolving into nothingness again. "It was not this creature's destiny to transform a second time," said the entity. "And so its time is done. Learn from the example, Toa."

Vakama loaded a weakness disk into his launcher and took aim. "The only thing we have learned is that you are as coldhearted as Makuta your master," he snarled, sending the Kanoka disk toward its target.

The entity watched the Kanoka's approach impassively. The disk struck him head-on and immediately disintegrated. "Master? I have no master. Can anyone hope to master a force of the universe? Take your foolish beliefs and begone, Toa. Do not tempt my wrath."

The entity punctuated his words with another jet of energized protodermis, this one aimed at Matau. Whenua tackled the Toa of Air just before the liquid would have struck. "Get down!"

"But I might have been — ouch! — transformed," said Matau as he hit the ground. "I could have become a new-power Toa."

Whenua glanced up at where the protodermis had struck the wall, eating it away. "You know, brother, sometimes I think you have all the common sense of that wall," he muttered, "and are at least twice as thick."

In rapid succession, the entity mutated worms, microbes, a dozen different creatures who in their natural form were no threat. But touched by the power of energized protodermis, they became monstrous versions of their former selves, each one strong enough to defeat a Toa.

The Toa Metru defended themselves, with

elemental and mask powers against the creations of the protodermis entity. At first, it seemed like they would be brought low by sheer numbers. But when Whenua's Mask of Night Vision succeeded in blinding a rock worm and driving it back below the surface, the others took heart. Inch by inch, they advanced on the creatures until the horrors had all fallen or fled.

With that conflict done, Vakama signaled for the Toa to spread out and surround the pool. He, Nuju, Onewa, and Nokama each took up a position in front of one of the chamber's four pillars. The entity made no effort to stop them.

"The wrath of a puddle," said Nuju. "That might be amusing. Show us, creature, just how angry a pail of water can become."

The entity hurled its substance forth again, but not at Nuju, past him. It struck the far wall, but this time it did not dissolve the stone. Instead, a bipedal creature of rock detached itself from the wall and lumbered toward the Toa of Ice.

"I think this is the part where we 'lesser beings' are supposed to scream and run away," said Onewa. "You know what we do with rock in Po-Metru, friend?"

The Toa of Stone sent his elemental powers against the entity's creation. Instantly, the legs crumbled beneath the rock monster. "We smash it."

Another wave of power and the arms detached neatly and fell to the floor. "We carve it."

A final burst of energy and the rock creature crumbled to dust. "And sometimes we just give up . . ." Onewa said. Concentrating, he drew the rock dust and shattered pieces back together to form a boulder. "And start over again."

Onewa folded his arms and looked at the protodermis entity. "But then, we're not on your level, are we?"

Something in Onewa's tone sparked anger in the entity. It hurled another blast of protodermis. Onewa dodged and it struck the pillar, devouring the stone. Vakama saw this and smiled.

"I would have thought a superior being would have better aim," he shouted. "Or do you only fight through pawns?"

The entity whirled and sent forth another blast, missing again and melting another pillar. Then it, too, smiled. "Ah. I see what you are doing. You would have me destroy all four pillars and bury us all."

"Well, bury *you*," said Matau. "Us, we are not much for rock-blankets."

"You're right," said Vakama. "You are wiser than we are, so there is no point in trying to trick you. And no *one* of us could ever hope to defeat you . . ."

The Toa Metru had come a long way together since defeating the Morbuzakh in Metru Nui. They had survived betrayal, stopped Makuta, and fought their way to a new island home and now back. So all knew Vakama's statement was not just mere words, but a call to action.

The Toa of Fire was first, triggering his rocket pack and heading for the ceiling. Onewa and Whenua were next, using their powers to call forth walls of earth and stone around the pool. As the entity brought them down, it found itself confronted by more barriers of rock and ice. High above, Matau and Nokama combined their powers to form a violent storm inside the cave. Forked lightning bolts struck near the pool, charring the stone floor.

The protodermis entity turned this way and that, unsure where to strike first. It could easily end the existence of any of these Toa, but where to concentrate its powers? Targeting one would leave it vulnerable to the efforts of the others, and though they could not harm him, they might somehow damage the pool.

Matau shot past, using his aero-slicer blades and power over wind to propel him through the air. The entity tracked him and launched a blast of protodermis at a point in front of the Toa of Air. Matau chuckled and made a 180-degree turn straight up, avoiding the stream, which instead hit the third pillar. The entity cried out in rage at the sight.

Vakama signaled the others to halt their actions. He descended to the ground, standing face to face with the entity, mere inches away. "One pillar left," said the Toa of Fire. "We could never have brought down four before you stopped us, but one? That we can do."

"Go ahead," sneered the entity. "Rain a thousand tons of rock upon me. I will burn my way through it and still repay your defiance."

Nuju walked over to join Vakama. "Perhaps. Or perhaps another of Makuta's interesting little projects is up above . . . a creature that eats energized protodermis would seem to suit his warped ends. Maybe you would like to study that specimen?"

Onewa leaned casually against the fine pillar. "Sounds interesting. Let's not keep the two of them apart."

"You are speaking without knowledge," said the entity. It did not sound as if it believed its own words.

"Then Onewa can bring down the rock and we can all find out," said Vakama. "Or we can make a trade. We get our vial of protodermis and walk out, unharmed, and no further damage gets done to your chamber."

The entity paused in thought. Then it

bowed its head slightly, and said, "Very well. As a superior being, I can afford to be . . . generous."

Vakama dipped the vial into the pool, emerging with a small amount of the precious liquid. Then he backed slowly away, never taking his eyes off the entity. When he and the other Toa were near the entrance, they turned and headed for the tunnel.

Nokama was the first to hear the rushing sound, as if a wall of water was heading toward them. She turned to see that the entity had formed itself into a tidal wave and was bearing down upon them. She shouted a warning, but by then the other Toa had sighted the danger as well. Onewa lashed out with his elemental energies and shattered the last pillar, bringing the stone ceiling crashing down.

The entity's substance hung suspended for only a moment, as if in shock. Then an avalanche of rock plummeted down upon it, the great weight breaking through the floor beneath. Safe in the tunnel, the Toa Metru watched as the entire chamber collapsed into the darkness.

"That's the problem with superior beings," said Onewa. "They lie a lot."

"Such a waste," Nokama said, shaking her head sadly. "Makuta, the Karzahni, and now this . . . so much power, so much knowledge, but no spirit — only the drive to destroy."

The Toa turned as one and walked quickly, leaving the chamber far behind them.

The Toa of Water could feel the "eyes" of the Karzahni upon her as they made their way back to its subterranean dwelling place. She could practically sense its anticipation as they drew nearer with the energized protodermis. Right then, she decided that she would not allow the others to bargain with that evil creature, even if it meant her own death.

The plant-thing's branches opened as if in welcome as they entered the cave. "I am amazed to see you have all survived," the Karzahni whispered.

"More than survived," said Vakama, producing the vial. "We have what you asked for. Now keep your word and cure Nokama."

The myriad parts of the Karzahni rustled. A vine reached out to snatch the vial away, but

Vakama pulled his hand back. "I gave you no word to keep," said the creature. "And I must test what you have brought me, mustn't I? Let me have it, or know that you have doomed your friend."

"As you're doomed?" asked Nuju. "This journey has not been what it seemed, from the beginning. We fought creatures we thought meant to harm us, but who only sought escape. And you, so sure of your power . . . you have little time left, isn't that right, Karzahni?"

The plant's appendages drew closer to the trunk, as if preparing for an attack. "You are very clever, Nuju. You should have been a Vahki."

"You said it yourself," Nuju replied. "Everything here is dying. Makuta designs his creations with a limited lifespan, doesn't he, so they can never be a threat to him."

The Karzahni laughed. "No, Toa of Ice. He simply does not want to be confronted by his 'failures' on and on, throughout the centuries. But with what is in that vial, I will surpass him. I will do all that he could not, and in the end, I will be the master and he the slave. Now give me that vial!"

Vakama lifted the tube of energized proto-dermis into the air and tilted it slightly, as if intending to pour it out on the ground. "I will test it for you."

"You wouldn't," snapped the Karzahni.

The Toa of Fire's smile sent a chill even through the other Toa. "Karzahni, after what I have been through these past weeks . . . there is very little I wouldn't do."

A portion of the ground erupted at the feet of Nokama. A small root forced its way up through the stone. "Eat of that," the Karzahni said to her, "and you will be healed. What one of Makuta's creations can do, another can undo."

Nokama hesitated. Perhaps this thing meant to poison her? But no, then its hold over the Toa Metru would be gone and her friends could safely flee with the vial. She knelt down, plucked the root, and placed it in her mouth. Its taste was bitter, yet she could already feel the strength flooding her limbs again. She looked up at Vakama and nodded.

The Toa of Fire extended the vial.

"Are you crazy?" said Onewa. "You can't give that kind of power to this thing!"

"Toa keep their word," Vakama replied. "Otherwise, we are no better than the things we fight."

The Karzahni's vine grabbed the vial and brought it close to the trunk. "Yes, it is the stuff of life," the plant creature said, voice bubbling with dark pleasure. "It will transform me into more than what I am. I will be free to walk, to grow, to conquer in ways my creator could only dream. Just a few drops . . ."

The Toa stood transfixed as the silver liquid splashed upon a branch of the Karzahni. For a moment, the entire plant seemed to sway as if caught in a gale wind. Then the vial was flung to the ground as the Karzahni screamed.

"It burns! It buuuuuurrrrrnnnnns!"

Chaos seized hold of the plant-thing, its

limbs spasming as the power of the energized protodermis coursed through it. Unlike the stone rat and the mutated insect, the Karzahni did not dissolve, but was instead ravaged by fires within. An acrid smell of dying plant flesh filled the air as one by one the monster's limbs decayed and dropped to the ground.

"This isn't what it thought-wished for, is it?" asked Matau.

"It was not the Karzahni's destiny to transform," answered Nuju. "That left only one other choice."

"This . . . this is horrible. Isn't there something we can do?" whispered Nokama.

Nuju shook his head. This was not a fate he would have wished even on Makuta, but the Karzahni had made its choice. It valued power even more than life, and so had lost both.

Then it was over. The withered, blackened form of the Karzahni sagged, with only its root structure embedded in the wall keeping it from hitting the ground. "Makuta's final jest," it said weakly, "the promise of eternal power masking the reality of doom."

"Yes," said Vakama. "Makuta has a fondness for . . . masks."

"I could still muster enough strength, somehow, to defeat you all," said the Karzahni. "But . . . I will not. Hear my words, Toa: You have not stopped Makuta, only slowed him. You return to a Metru Nui much changed, and for the worse. Only fear and disaster wait for you there. But I will let you go . . . for only Toa can hope to bring an end to my creator. And . . . he must be . . . ended."

Then the Karzahni spoke no more. Nuju inspected the creature for a moment before turning to the others. "The power of the protodermis has consumed it," he said. "Like Ahkmou, like Mavrah, like too many others, all victims of the darkness within them."

Vakama knew he should say something. Wise and reassuring words were what were needed, but none came to him. Instead, he felt a great weariness. Being a Toa, it seemed, meant facing the darkness and overcoming it, time after time.

But what of the ones of whom Nuju spoke? he wondered. *What must it be like to fall before the darkness inside yourself?*

The Toa of Fire hoped and prayed that none of them would ever find out.

EPILOGUE

"The telling of the tale is done," said Turaga Vakama, his voice barely more than a whisper. "In time, we made our way back to the shores of the silver sea. Metru Nui lay before us, filled with Matoran trapped in endless sleep."

He rose, using his staff to support himself. "Before his death, Toa Lhikan had asked that we safeguard the heart of Metru Nui. That heart was the Matoran. Now we were prepared to enter our wounded city and save them all. Our moment of destiny was at hand."

Vakama's eyes met Tahu Nuva's. "And now I have told all that I wish to . . . perhaps all that I dare. You know what I must now ask, Tahu."

The Toa Nuva of Fire rose. "Then you must also know my answer, Turaga."

The other Turaga present rose in protest, but Vakama gestured for them to be silent. "It is decided then. But, hear me, Tahu — I will share my tale with you, and only you. Then you must decide if other ears can bear to hear."

"More secrets, Turaga?"

Vakama bowed his head and walked slowly away. "There are some words never meant to be uttered, Toa Tahu," he said. "There are some stories never meant to be told."